To Ray
I love thee to the level of every day's most quiet need.
—L. K.

To Emiline
—L. M.

How Do I Love You?
Text copyright © 2006 by Leslie Kimmelman Illustrations copyright © 2006 by Lisa McCue
Manufactured in China. All rights reserved. No part of this book may be used or reproduced in any
manner whatsoever without written permission except in the case of brief quotations embodied in
critical articles and reviews. For information address HarperCollins Children's Books, a division of
HarperCollins Publishers, 1350 Avenue of the Americas, New York, NY 10019.
www.harperchildrens.com

Library of Congress Cataloging-in-Publication Data
Kimmelman, Leslie.   How do I love you? / by Leslie Kimmelman ; illustrated by Lisa McCue.
— 1st ed.   p. cm.
Summary: Counts the ways in which a child can be loved, from one to twenty and more.
ISBN-10: 0-06-001200-5 — ISBN-10: 0-06-001201-3 (lib. bdg.)
ISBN-13: 978-0-06-001200-7 — ISBN-13: 978-0-06-001201-4 (lib. bdg.)
[1. Love—Fiction. 2. Counting. 3. Stories in rhyme.] I. McCue, Lisa, ill. II. Title.
PZ8.3.K5598How 2006   2003026558   [E]—dc22   CIP   AC

Typography by Amelia May Anderson
3 4 5 6 7 8 9 10
❖ First Edition

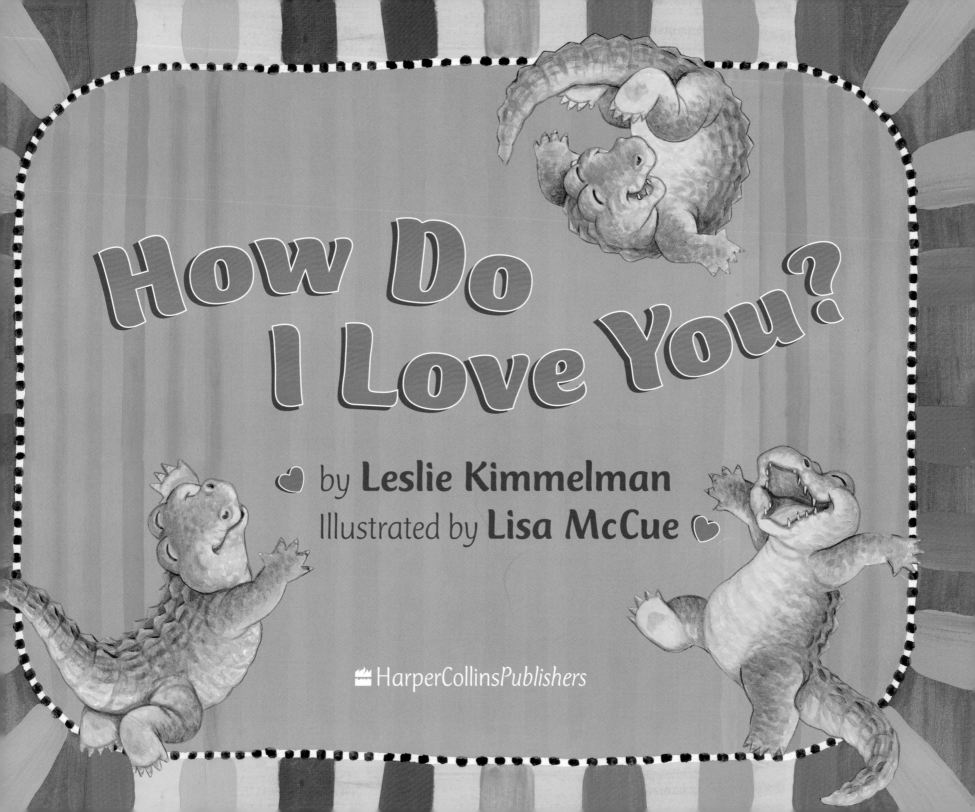

How Do I Love You?

♥ by **Leslie Kimmelman**

Illustrated by **Lisa McCue** ♥

HarperCollinsPublishers

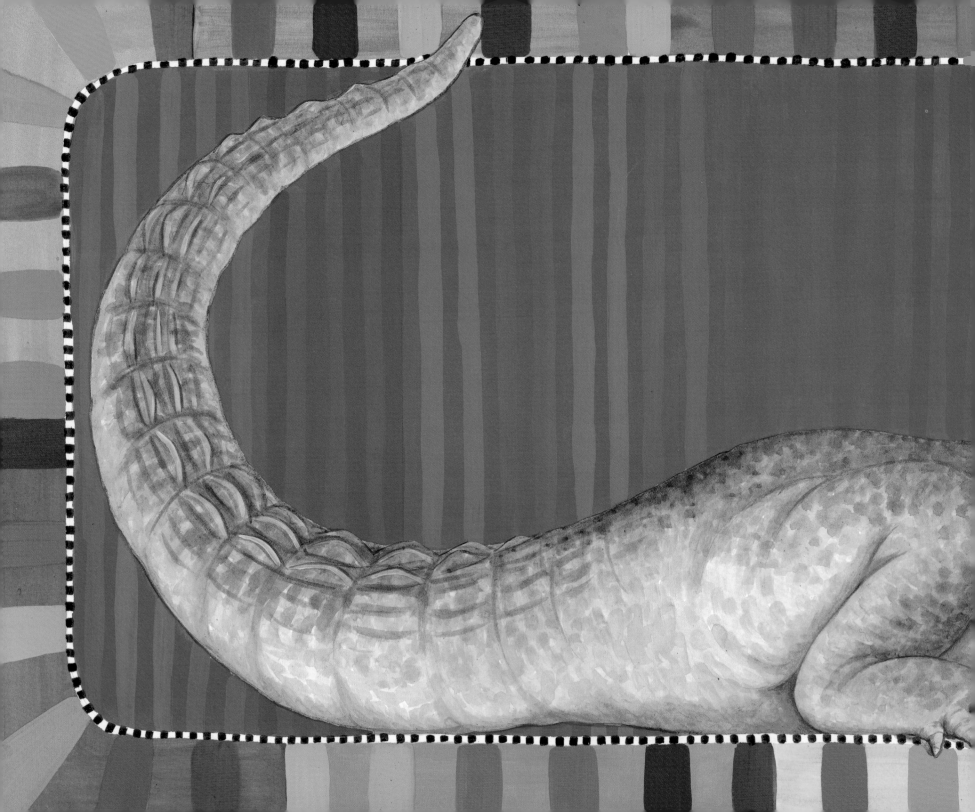

How do I love you, little one?
Let me count the ways. . . .

One in sunshine;

Two in snow;

Three on rainy days.

Four I love you
right side up,

Five and upside down.

Six I love your happy smile;

I even love your frown.

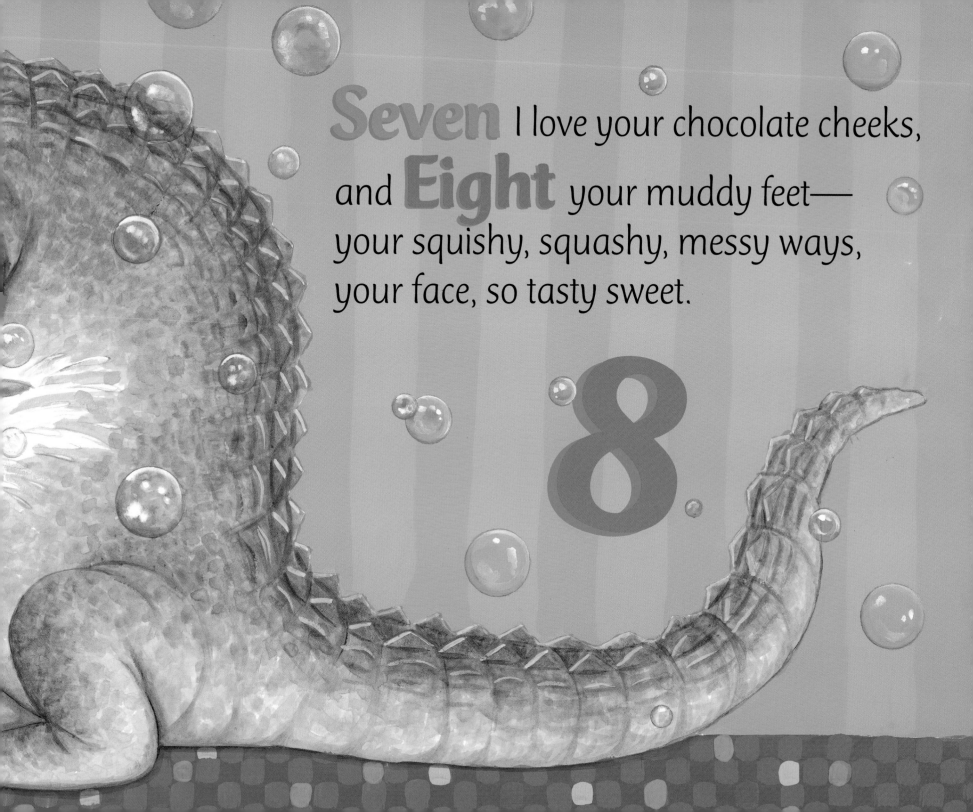

Seven I love your chocolate cheeks,
and **Eight** your muddy feet—
your squishy, squashy, messy ways,
your face, so tasty sweet.

8

Nine I love when we jump waves
each summer at the shore;
and search for seashells—that makes **Ten**

10

Let's count a little more.

Eleven

I love your pictures;
I hang them on the wall.

Twelve I'll love you when you're grown;

Thirteen I love you small.

13

14

15

Fourteen

Fifteen

Sixteen

each silly dance you do,
or spin you spin, or grin you grin
when you try something new.

I love you morning, noon, and night—
that's number **Seventeen**:

in summer, autumn, winter, spring,
and each day in between.

Eighteen I love you 'neath the moon that shines when day is done,

18

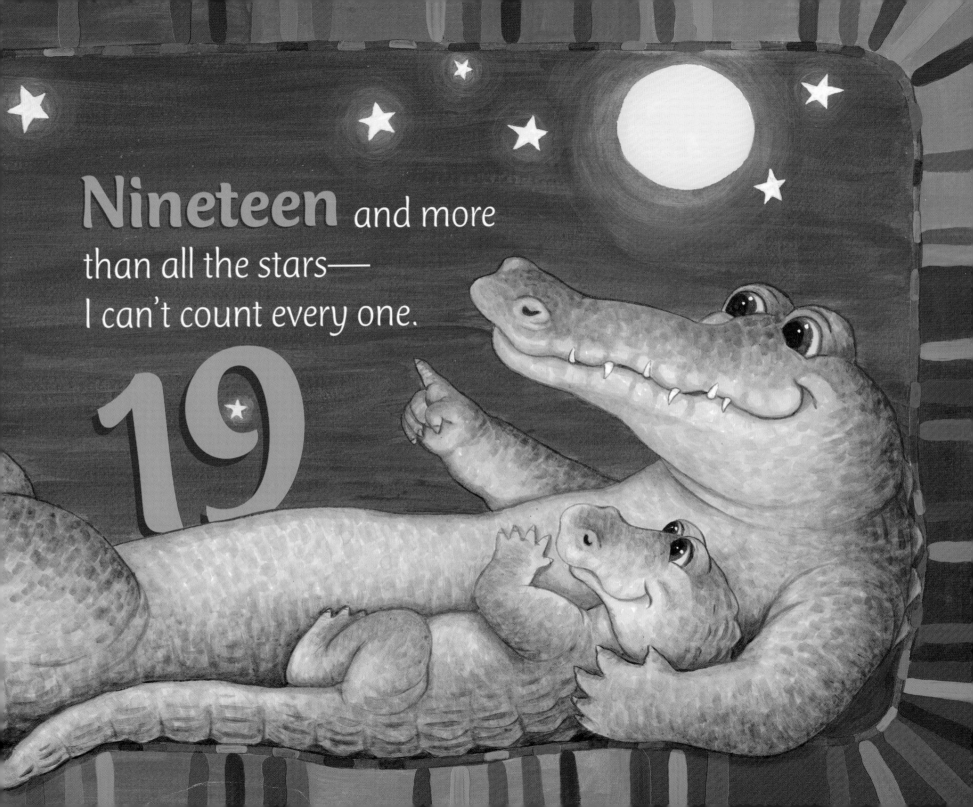

Nineteen and more
than all the stars—
I can't count every one.

19

I really love to count with you,
and up to **Twenty**'s tough.
But when it comes to loving you,
well, twenty's not enough.

20